SNOWDEER

To Louise + Ron
God bless
Love,
Randy Plummer

by Randy Plummer

© 2011 Randy Plummer

DEDICATION

I would like to dedicate SNOWDEER in honor of my grandparents, Lester and Evelyn Plummer, who we called Papa and Mommom. They are represented by Mommom and Papa Whitetail in the story.

I also dedicate SNOWDEER to my parents, Darrell and Rosie Plummer, who are Darrell and Rose Marie (Plum Puddin's parents) in the Story.

And last, but not least, I want to dedicate SNOWDEER to my aunt and uncle, Jim and Delores Plummer who are SNOWDEER's parents, Jim-Buck and Deerlores.

ACKNOWLEDGEMENTS

I want to Thank Raine Clotfelter for creating the beautiful painting of SNOWDEER, and Thanks also to Ken Craig for all of his creative ideas.

CHAPTER ONE

Grandpa Deer reads to his granddeer

Once upon a time, on Christmas eve, Grandpa Deer is up in a bedroom in his log cabin reading a book to his granddeer, who are lying in their beds listening intently. He reads, *"once upon a time many years ago, there was a young buck by the name of Snowdeer. He and his family lived in a part of the forest called Doe Run. This family of deer had a normal happy life, but this Christmas, special things would happen that would change their lives forever."*

As Grandpa keeps reading, his voice fades as we hear from the outside a snowstorm coming. As snowflakes blow across the sky we see that some of the flakes have smiling faces and some with mischievous faces and others are laughing. We follow them as they keep blowing thru the night.

But then, it gets lighter and lighter and the snow blows on to the north and reveals the daylight and once upon a time in the woods where a little white buck is standing with his mother and grandmother.

CHAPTER TWO

Snowdeer, Deerlores, Mommom Whitetail, and past Christmas memories

"Momma, how close is it to Christmas?" asks Snowdeer. "Here in the forest it sure looks like it's gonna snow and I can't wait!"

His mother, Deerlores says to Snowdeer, "I know Snowdeer, it does look like it's going to snow, and your daddy, Jim-Buck, is out gathering nuts and berries and anything else he can find to feed us and when he comes back he will know if it will snow soon. He seems to have a gift of knowing how the weather will fall. Speaking of fall, most of the leaves have all fallen now and we can see thru the forest so easily. Isn't it beautiful Snowdeer?"

"Yes, mama it is," Snowdeer answers. And then, he turns and asks his grandma, Evelyn Whitetail, "what do you think Mommom Whitetail?"

Mommom Whitetail is crocheting a rug and stops to answer Snowdeer's question. "I agree with you both Snowdeer, and Deerlores, it is beautiful. I have always loved this time of year so much. I can find my way around the woods a lot better and I can keep a sharper eye on the little ones," she laughs.

Deerlores laughs and says, "Snowdeer, I have some exciting news for you. Thanksgiving was just here and took place in a month humans call November, and it is now the month the humans call December and Christmas is in this month!"

Mommom Whitetail breaks in and says, "oh, how I love Christmas time! I could celebrate it every day!"

Deerlores continues, "matter of fact, today it is December 23rd, and only 2 days till Christmas, and once again, us animals celebrate it too! God created all of us—humans and animals alike—and we all celebrate his son's birthday in our own special way. I remember when I was your age how I loved Christmas, and how in the middle of the forest, Mom and Daddy Deer would find a perfect cedar tree. Why I bet the trees they found were at least 15 feet tall!"

"Yeah, what fond memories, Deerlores," says Mommom Whitetail. "Snowdeer, I remember when we did that with your daddy, Jim-Buck, as well. What did you and your mom and dad put on your tree, Deerlores?"

Deerlores excitedly recalls, "we would put berries, acorns, persimmons, wild grapes, hickory nuts and apples on it, and wrap blades of grass in a circle and tie them together and they would make Christmas rings and hang them all over the tree. The Christmas colors of red and green added the perfect look. I would get so excited and all our animal friends here in Doe Run would dance and sing Christmas carols around the beautiful tree. Then on Christmas day, our gift to each other was to feast on the decorations!

"Yea, I couldn't wait for Christmas day either—the best day of the year, and we didn't have to cook!" laughs Mommom Whitetail.

Deerlores then says, "the great part about our Christmas tree is that it was always in the woods and that gave us Christmas memories all year long. You know after we met our human friend, Plum Puddin' right after he was born—along with his dog Pinecone, his father Darrell and his mother Rose Marie, we would do the same thing. But only this time, we could share with animals and humans alike. We truly felt like family at that wonderful Christmas time of year. It has been a long time since we have done that."

Snowdeer excitedly says, "wow…that sounds great momma! Let's do it this year! The other Christmases I remember have all been great, but to decorate a Cedar tree like you did when you were a little doe, and have our animal and our human friends come and celebrate and sing about Christmas sounds so wonderful! And to get to eat the decorations! Two hooves way up!!! It makes me want to go into our happy hoof dance momma!" Snowdeer laughs and raises his front two hooves, and Deerlores raises her front hooves up and they do a high-5 and dance around doing their happy hoof dance.

Mommom Whitetail says, "well, Deerlores, Snowdeer, I'm gonna shake a hoof myself and get back to Knob Lick before it gets dark. Gonna go get supper ready for Papa Whitetail. He'll be coming in from the barn where he's been putting feed and hay out for the animals and gathering eggs. See you all soon. Merry Christmas!"

"Goodbye Mommom Whitetail, Merry Christmas, and see you in a couple of days! Tell Papa Whitetail Merry Christmas! Love you," says Snowdeer.

"Love you too, Snowdeer," answers Mommom Whitetail as she heads thru the woods.

Snowdeer then says, "Momma, let's get in touch with Plum Puddin' since we haven't celebrated Christmas with them in a few years. Maybe they will come and celebrate with us this year!"

"Okay, I would love to do that," says Deerlores.

CHAPTER THREE

Deerlores tells Snowdeer Plum Puddin's secret with Santa

"Snowdeer, did I ever tell you about Plum Puddin' and his special secret with Santa?"

"No, momma you hadn't. Please tell me!"

"Well," she continues, "once upon a time, when Plum Puddin' was a baby, his mother made him plum pudding all the time. She had a secret recipe and cooked it on the hearth at the fireplace inside their log cabin over in Possum Holler by Knob Lick. He loved the plum pudding so much that they nicknamed him Plum Puddin'. His real name is Randy but Plum Puddin' just kinda stuck, and that's what everybody called him and they continue to call him that to this day. Now it wouldn't be right calling him anything else! Plum Puddin' is a special name, and Snowdeer, you also have a special name. You were born at Christmas time during one of our biggest and most beautiful snows. You were born solid white, and with you being so pretty and white and the snow being so pretty and white—I called you Snowdeer—in honor of our beautiful snow.

Snowdeer excitedly says, "wow, I was named after the snow! Thank you momma, you and daddy deer are the best!"

Deerlores continues, "I wanted to let you know at just the perfect time, and now seemed to be the time. You are special Snowdeer, not just in the color of your fur, but you as a deer. I believe you will have many special things happen in your life, and I want to see everyone of them because your dad and I love you very much.

Snowdeer and Deerlores stand close and Snowdeer puts his head against Deerlores's neck…then Deerlores remembers. "Oh, before I forget, I had one more story to tell you about Plum Puddin'. When Plum Puddin' got old enough to write letters to Santa, he got an idea to send Santa a special jar of Plum Puddin' that his momma made along with a Christmas note. Santa received it on the 23rd of December. Then, for Christmas that year, when Santa was delivering Christmas presents, he put in Plum Puddin's stocking a magical jar—studded with diamonds—along with a note that said whenever Plum Puddin' opens it, and says he wishes to see Santa, it would magically take him and Pinecone, his dog to Santa's village at the North Pole. Now, every December 23rd, Plum Puddin' takes his annual trip to Santa to take a jar of his mommas plum pudding in that special diamond jar and he visits Mrs. Santa, Josh, Harvey and the other elves and the reindeer."

"Wow momma! I didn't know that! And it is December 23rd right now! He will be leaving tonight to go see Santa! We just gotta have Plum Puddin' come for Christmas this year! He can tell us what is going on at the North Pole 'cause he will have just been there! Maybe he will bring us some of his mother's plum pudding for us to eat too! Even though it isn't Christmas yet, it feels like I'm having Christmas on the inside!"

Deerlores laughs and says, "me too, my little deer."

"Ah, momma, please don't call me *little dear*…why I am already 7 years old!"

Deerlores laughs and then Snowdeer begins to laugh too and starts looking upward toward Santa's and the North Pole and gets very quiet.

Deerlores sees Snowdeer is upset and asks, "what's wrong Snowdeer? You were just jumping for joy-now you're very quiet. Is there something bothering you?"

"Yes momma there is… It has been on my mind for a long time. Matter of fact, ever since last Christmas and the Christmas before that and the Christmas before that and the Christmas before… Anyway, as far back as I can remember…"

Deerlores breaks in and asks in a serious caring voice, "Snowdeer, what is it?"

Snowdeer replies, "what I have been wondering is well, it's about Santa Claus. Santa has been bringing gifts to humans and to us here in Doe Run ever since I have been born, and even before I was born is what you have told me. You also said that Plum Puddin' and his family are the only humans that know that Santa delivers to us out here in the woods as well as going down the chimney to take presents to those who are nice and not naughty."

"Yes, that is all true, Snowdeer, but you still haven't told me what is bothering you. Come on, you can tell your momma what's wrong and I promise not to laugh or make fun of what you tell me."

Snowdeer gets a funny look on his face and then decides just to tell his mom everything on his heart. He becomes more confident and opens up and says, "Okay, this is what I am wondering. Santa flies every year with his sleigh and that big bag full of presents and all his reindeer."

"Yes, that's right," says Deerlores.

Snowdeer continues, "well, what I want for my Christmas gift this year is for Santa to pick us to fly him around the world to deliver presents-just for one night—that's all I want! I promise I won't ask for any other gift."

Deerlores, being surprised says, "why Snowdeer, that would be wonderful but what would Santa do with his reindeer? For centuries they have been so used to leading Santa's sleigh. What would they do?"

"I know momma, but I was just thinking-wouldn't it be nice…"

Then Deerlores says, "wait Snowdeer, I think I hear your father coming. I can tell by the way he walks thru the rustling of the leaves. Tell him about your wish for Christmas."

They listen as Jim-Buck and Snowdeer's brothers and sister walk up to them, hooves rustling the leaves.

"Hello daddy, hello Longnose, Antler, and everybody! Glad you're home!" says Snowdeer.

"How was your day of berry picking?" Deerlores asks.

Jim-buck smiles and says, "hello everyone! We had a great day! Got lots of berries, apples, nuts, and other goodies for you, Snowdeer, Deerell, Rosie, Longnose, Antler, and the others in the family that will be here on Christmas. Now we have enough to get us through the Christmas season and into the new year."

Antler jokes and says, "we should have enough... we picked enough nuts and berries to feed all of "buck"-ingham palace! Ha ha.

"Longnose chimes in and says, "Antler, you oughten not "horn" in while daddy-buck's talkin'! Ha ha."

Deerell, Snowdeer's brother says, "in that case, the buck stops here!"

They all break into laughter and then Snowdeer's sister Rosie says, "Deerell, you're gonna get us skinned! Ha ha."

Jim-Buck clears his throat to let them know he was interrupted— but in a fun way and then continues... "the snowfall is coming very soon but now we won't have to go out looking for food. I have sure missed you all and speaking of missing you all, have I missed anything exciting since I left?"

"Yes, you certainly have, Jim-Buck," says Deerlores. "Snowdeer has a very special Christmas present he wants this year."

"Oh? What's that?" asks Jim-Buck.

Deerlores says, "Snowdeer, go ahead and tell your father."

Then Snowdeer says, "Okay, I just told momma for my Christmas present from Santa this year, I want him to use *us* to pull his sleigh. Wouldn't it be fun to soar thru the sky knowing we were delivering Christmas presents with Santa to all of the humans and animals on earth?"

Jim-buck raises his head back and says, "whoa! That's a big request Snowdeer! I don't know 'bout that! You do realize that has never been done before and I don't know if Santa would ever allow it. You see his reindeer team has been faithful for many, many years and he wouldn't want to take away their fun of delivering presents Christmas eve. Plus, it's a long way from Doe Run to the North Pole. However, the thought does sound inviting and a whole lot of fun!"

Jim-buck chuckles at the idea of being one of Santa's team, when Deerlores says, "now Jim-Buck, it does sound like fun, I admit, but let's be practical. Don't lead your son on just to be let down."

"Ah, dear it doesn't hurt to have dreams for something, even if that something has never been done before," Jim-Buck says."I know we could do it but the only thing is…well…"

Snowdeer excitedly says, "what daddy, what?"

"Well, Snowdeer, we would need, "deer tags" to be able to drive Santa's sleigh!!!! Hahahahaha"

Once again, they all break into laughter and when Jim-Buck snorts, that brings more laughter and then he says, "nothing like a good buck snort! That's what your uncle Ken-Buck always says! Hey, there's Ken-Buck over there, right now!"

They all look over in a nearby group of hickory nut trees and see uncle Ken-Buck with his face in the leaves trying to find some fallen hickory nuts to eat.

"Isn't uncle Ken-Buck cool?" says Snowdeer.

Jim-Buck who is Ken-Bucks brother replies, "he is for sure cool, Snowdeer. I know you always admired him because he brings you nuts and berries and also 'cause he is the only one in the family who wears a beard and mustache."

Ken-buck happens to look over their way and realizes they are looking at him. He waves his hoof at them, but when he looks up, they see leaves and stickers have stuck to his face giving him a very "fall" looking mustache. He then realizes he has this on himself and begins blowing and snorting trying to get it off.

Snowdeer and the family start laughing, and Ken-Buck shakes his head at them and goes right back to eating and getting it all back on his beard and mustache again.

Snowdeer has laughed so hard he has fallen in a leaf pile rolling and snorting. When they settle down, Snowdeer looks up and you can't see his body, for he's covered with leaves and only his blue eyes are shining thru.

Jim-Buck says to Snowdeer, "well, son, if I were you, I think I would put your special Christmas wish on a letter to Santa. It's only 2 days till Christmas, so I would send him a letter right now. You know he gets millions of them every year from children and animals alike. The sooner you send it—the sooner he sees it and can think about your wish."

Snowdeer is now all excited and says, "yea! That is exactly what I will do! Momma, can you help me write the letter to Santa please?"

Deerlores says, "why sure, my little deer."

Snowdeer, once again annoyed by being called little deer says, "momma, there you go again."

Deerlores laughs and says, "I know, I know, it was just too good to leave unsaid!"

Jim-Buck, getting excited with another idea says, "hey Snowdeer I have a great "ideer"!"

After they bust out in laughter again, Jim-Buck says, "after you get your letter to Santa written, why don't you go visit Plum Puddin' and ask him if he will take it directly to Santa when he goes to take plum pudding to him tonight!"

Snowdeer, overjoyed, says, "that's a great idea daddy! Let's go momma and get that letter written to Santa!"

CHAPTER FOUR

Plum Puddin' prepares plum pudding at his cabin.

Meanwhile, in the woods of Possum Holler by Knob Lick, Plum Puddin' is in his cabin alone with Pinecone, his dog. His parents, Darrell, and Rose Marie, have left to visit relatives in Knob Lick.

Plum Puddin' decides to take his mother's recipe and make a batch of plum pudding himself. He has it all made and is filling jars. Then he says to Pinecone, "Are you ready, Pinecone?" Pinecone wags his tail, puts his front paws on Plum Puddin's knees, and does an excited whimper. "Okay, here we go! Now to fill the magical plum pudding jar for Santa!" Pinecone wags his tail even more and his excited whimper gets louder and then he starts to bark.

Plum Puddin' goes to the special cupboard where sits the magical jar that Santa gave him. When he opens the cupboard, the light from the magical jar shines so bright from the diamonds that are on it that Plum Puddin' has to squint his eyes! The jar also has a solid golden lid on it with an "S" written in red on top for Santa.

Plum Puddin' reaches for the jar then takes it to the hearth and begins to fill it. He knows once he fills it and screws the lid on nice and tight and holds it in his right hand, all he has to say is the magic words Santa gave him and he will be taken to the North Pole to see the Clauses. The magic words Santa gave Plum Puddin' are, "Ho Ho Ho, off to the North Pole we go!"

Plum Puddin' once again looks at Pinecone and says, "Pinecone, the best plum pudding is always at the bottom of the kettle and I like to save that for Santa. I'll fill Santa's magical jar- then let's head to the North Pole!"

Pinecone barks loud again, and after Plum Puddin' has put the last dip of plum pudding in, he takes a quick taste from the spoon then tightens the golden lid. The jar beams brightly from the beautiful diamonds, but when plum pudding is added it takes on an even brighter glow!

Plum Puddin' smiles big and Pinecone barks and jumps up and down!

Then, all of a sudden, he hears a knock at the cabin door. He goes to the door holding the magical jar of plum pudding. When he opens the door, he sees Snowdeer standing there with his special Christmas wish letter for Santa.

"Snowdeer! So great to see you! I've missed you! Been wanting to walk thru the woods to visit you."

Snowdeer says, "I've missed you too, Plum Puddin'! Momma deer just told me how you got your name and all about you and Santa's secret! I promise I won't tell!"

Staring at Plum Puddin's magical glowing jar, Snowdeer says, "that jar of plum pudding is so bright! Is that the jar Santa gave you?"

"Yes, it is Snowdeer," says Plum Puddin'. "Every year I travel to the North Pole to see Santa. Take him a fresh batch of Plum Puddin' in this magical jar. Then Santa brings this magical jar back to me along with my present. Getting ready to head out tonight. Can't hardly wait to see Santa, Mrs. Santa, and the gang!"

Snowdeer, still enchanted with Plum Puddin's pudding jar says, "I bet you are excited! Wow! Wish I could go!"

Plum Puddin' sees Snowdeer's excitement, and says, "you know Snowdeer, when I am up at Santa's, I'll ask if you can come with me in the future. I'd love to have you go with me. You won't believe what all he has up there! There are elves all over the place!"

This only makes Snowdeer even more excited and he says, "wow, I wanna go now" and then says, "hey, Plum Puddin' I have a special favor to ask of you. I've written my Christmas wish letter to Santa. Could you take it to him tonight when you go see him? I have a special Christmas wish I just got to get it to him!"

Plum Puddin' says, "sure, I'll gladly take it to him! Santa loves getting Christmas wish letters from animals and humans all around the world. He told me once that one of his favorite things to do is to sit in his hightop chair, drink hot cocoa, and read the many letters he gets. Did you know he even gets Christmas wish lists as early as Easter? I guess some people like to spread Christmas out!"

Snowdeer, laughing says, "Yea, I agree with that one!"

Snowdeer, knowing that Plum Puddin' is excited to head to the North Pole, decides to leave, but first he says, "thanks Plum Puddin', for delivering my letter to Santa. Have a great trip. Oh, before I forget, I and the family want you all to come over Christmas day. We're gonna have all kinds of goodies. Would you care bringing some plum pudding please?"

Plum Puddin' laughingly says, "we would love to come and celebrate Christmas day with you. For the first time, I made plum pudding myself and I'm gonna take some of it to Santa and see what he thinks. What left over pudding I have I'll bring over to your cabin Christmas day!"

"That sounds great Plum," says Snowdeer. "See you in two days! Bye!"

"Bye Snowdeer," Plum Puddin' answers, and then excitedly looks down at Pinecone and grabs the magical jar of plum pudding with his right hand and says, "are you ready Pinecone?"

Pinecone, knowing what is going to take place, barks loudly back to Plum Puddin'.

Plum Puddin' then joyfully says those magic words Santa gave him…

"Ho Ho Ho! Off to the North Pole we go!"

With a wishk, woosh, whouse, there was nobody left in the house, except in the corner there sat a little confused mouse. Later that evening back at Doe Run, after Snowdeer had gone to bed, Jim-Buck and Deerlores discuss Snowdeer's wish to drive Santa's sleigh.

Deerlores says, "I hope we didn't build Snowdeer's hopes too high, in case Santa doesn't give him his wish. I think down deep inside he knows that his wish can't be filled."

Jim-Buck doesn't feel the same and says, "Dear, I don't think Snowdeer's going to take 'no' for an answer. He really does believe Santa will come thru with his wish."

CHAPTER FIVE

Santa, Mrs. Santa, and the North Pole

Meanwhile, we find Santa and Mrs. Santa, up at the North Pole. It is cold, and the wind is blowing, and Christmas time fills the air…

Santa is all excited about going out with his reindeer team once again, and he says to Mrs. Claus, "Ho Ho Ho, well, Christmas is coming soon Mrs. Claus. What do you want for Christmas this year?"

Mrs. Santa lovingly says, "the same thing I have asked for hundreds and hundreds of years…that you will bring joy and happiness to millions of boys and girls and animals this Christmas Season, and that you will be safe. You know Mr. Claus you have been flying a long time, and you have a perfect track record and you and none of your reindeer have ever gotten sick on Christmas. Everything has been right on schedule."

Santa answers, "yes, you are right Mrs. Claus. God has been good to us, and I am hoping that tomorrow night we can add another perfect night to our list of successful flights! Hey, did I see your name on the naughty list this year? Will it be coal in your stocking this Christmas Mrs. C? Ho Ho Ho!"

Mrs. Claus comes right back at him joking and says, "I don't think so. Having to put up with you for 365 days a year, I think *I* deserve a vacation to the south pole! Ho Ho Ho," she says in a fun, sarcastic voice.

"That's my girl! Always perfect, always a step ahead and always plump! Ho Ho Ho."

Mrs. Claus once again comes right back at him and says, "Now *that* comment will put *you* on the naughty list, Mr. Belly like a bowlful of jelly! Ho Ho Ho."

Santa does a belly laugh and says, "okay, I give in—you win! Hey, speaking of a bowlful of jelly, I wonder if Plum Puddin' will make it up here to the North Pole this Christmas? I would love to see him and I have been so hungry for some of his mother's plum pudding!"

"I sure hope so Santa! I have been wanting some plum pudding too!"

Chapter Six

Plum Puddin' and Pinecone arrive at the North Pole's pole.

Santa and Mrs. Santa didn't know it yet, but Plum Puddin' and Pinecone have already been taken magically to the North Pole. They look around, marveling at Santa's village, and seeing Santa's magical sugar snow falling there at the North Pole's pole. They see a light coming down from Heaven, shining on the sugar snow as it falls. Plum Puddin' is holding the magical jar Santa gave him that is filled with plum pudding. He has a cloth around his neck like a sling that holds his own jar of plum pudding, and he has *plum pudding* written on the side of the jar. Every once in a while, plum pudding drips out from the jar and Pinecone catches the drops with his tongue.

They start heading towards the Claus's house, walking by the reindeer barn and seeing thousands of elves at different locations. There are elves stringing Christmas lights, garland, and tinsel on trees and on buildings. They giggle as they catch a few elf couples kissing underneath the mistletoe.

They see elves throwing snowballs and even an elf working at a snowcone stand with different colored toppings. Plum Puddin' reads the fun names of businesses written on their buildings and on their shop windows, like... *Grandpa Davis Candy Cane Factory, Plummer's Reindeer Hardware, Herschends Chocolate Factory, Carron's Kettle Corn, Mick's Elfwear, Taneyelf Country Store, Krull's Confectionary, Body by Dorn Health and Fitness, Marquarts Molasses, Melodydale's Music Store, and Raisin' Cane Baby Sitter Services.* They even have a local elf's club!

There are also decorated street signs at every corner, with some of the names being, *Hustle and Bustle, Holly and Vine, Ron and JoAnn, and Egg Nog and Thyme.*

Plum Puddin' walks by and sees Strike the Bell and gives a loud, "hello, Strike!!!"

Strike smiles, and then rings a Christmas greeting back at them.

They walk past Josh, the singing elf, who is leaning against a building singing and playing his guitar. Josh is there along with his singing buddy, Branson the Balladeer—a real singing deer.

Plum Puddin' greets them with a " Merry Christmas Josh and Branson"!

Josh waves at them and Branson raises a hoof to wave while they are singing.

Plum Puddin' walks by and hears JB, the disc jockey elf, playing music and hears JB say, "welcome to the crystal clear Christmas sounds of "CMAS" coming to you live from the North Pole and reaching around the world from the North Pole to the South Pole to all the good girls and boys."

JB sees Plum Puddin' and Pinecone and says… "Hey, Plum Puddin' and Pinecone! Welcome back to the North Pole! I'm doing a live broadcast from here at Santa's village. Want to say something to our listeners?"

Plum Puddin', being excited to send a Christmas greeting live from the North Pole out to the whole world says, "Merry, Merry Christmas to you! Hope all your season's dreams come true!"

JB the dj says, "thanks Plum Puddin'. You have a word for us Pinecone?"

Pinecone, in his best bark says, "ruff ruff!"

JB and Plum Puddin' laugh and JB says, "well, I guess ole Pinecone said it all! Haha"

Then Plum Puddin' says, "thanks JB! Merry Christmas! Tell Gina, Michael, and Kaethe Elf I said hello!"

JB says, "will do Plum! God's greatest to you!"

"You too JB," says Plum Puddin'.

As Plum Puddin' and Pinecone continue walking toward Santa's, they come upon Harvey, the reindeer preparation elf. He is in a hurry to get to the reindeer barn. Harvey passes them and then stops and skids after he realizes it is Plum Puddin' and Pinecone. He runs up to them, thrilled to see them.

Plum Puddin' says, "hello Harvey! How are you tonight?"

Harvey all out of breath from running says, "doing great Plum! Getting the reindeer ready for takeoff tomorrow night! I'm on my way to the reindeer barn to feed and water them. They're going to bed early tonight. They have a long day and night ahead of them! Oh, I see you brought plum pudding again this year! Santa and Mrs. Santa are gonna love it! Tell them to save me some this time!!! Ha Ha Ha Ho Ho Ho!!!"

Plum Puddin' laughs and he and Pinecone start walking again toward Santa's cottage. He gives Christmas greetings to other elves and looks over and sees his friends Jennie-elf and Gary-elf, teeter-tottering along with Donn-elf and Gaylene-elf. The North Pole has the largest playground in the world with enough swings, trampolines, ice skating rinks and brightly colored criss-crossing sliding boards to hold thousands of elves! They are laughing and joyful, and they all know Plum Puddin' and Pinecone.

They pass by the First Elfbyterian Church, and walk up to a stained glass window that is open a little bit and listen to their sweet voices as they have Christmas carol rehearsal. The closer they get to the Clauses, the more excited they become.

CHAPTER SEVEN

Plum Puddin' and Pinecone arrive at Santa's cottage.

As they arrive at Santa's cottage, Plum Puddin' says, "Pinecone, would you ring Santa's doorbell please?"

Pinecone goes up with his two front paws and rings the doorbell with his nose. When the doorbell rings, it plays a Christmas carol, which brings a smile to Plum Puddin's face and a wag to Pinecones tail.

The Clauses excitedly go to the door and find Plum Puddin' and Pinecone all smiles and holding a fresh batch of plum pudding inside the bright magical jar, still nice and warm from his mothers fireplace where he has cooked it.

Santa gives them a warm Christmas greeting saying, "welcome Plum Puddin' and Pinecone! Welcome! Mrs. Claus and I have missed you and your delicious plum pudding! Ho Ho Ho!"

Mrs. Claus hugs Plum Puddin', and Pinecone jumps up in Santa's arms, barking a Christmas greeting back to him.

Plum Puddin' says, "Merry Christmas Santa and Mrs. Santa! It's wonderful to see you both again! Here's a new batch of plum pudding, still hot from the hearth! I almost ate it before I got here! Haha just kiddin' ya!" Plum Puddin' hands the jar of plum pudding to the Clauses, and then says, "Daddy Darrell and Mama Rose Marie, send their Christmas greetings. Are you ready for takeoff tomorrow night?"

Santa says, "ready as I will ever be. Everything is on go!"

"Great, Santa," says Plum Puddin', "I live for this time of year, and getting to come up and visit you and the gang!"

CHAPTER EIGHT

Josh, Harvey and Branson the Balladeer at the reindeer barn

While Santa, Mrs. Santa and Plum Puddin' have been visiting, over in the reindeer barn Harvey—who Plum Puddin' ran into earlier, is working in the reindeer stable. He's been feeding and watering the reindeer. Now, after having bathed and brushed them all, they have all fallen asleep.

Josh, the singing elf and Branson the Balladeer, are there leading all of the elves in singing Christmas carols. After they finish a beautiful version of Joy to the World, Josh picks at Harvey the elf and says, "hey Harvey, I'll play, *There's a whole lota elfin' goin on,* and you can be Elfvis!"

They laugh and laugh and then Branson the Balladeer says, "hey, I have some of my original songs— I won't bore you with a bunch of them— I only have 50 or so, and they are all good. Can I sing them now?"

Knowing that this could take awhile, Josh says, "Ahhhhhhh…well…ahhhh, I would love to hear all of them right now, but I need to head over to the house. Mallory has been baking Christmas cookies and making candy and putting them in Christmas tins to send out with Santa, and I don't want to miss out eating some of them before they leave! There's nothing like a warm cookie and a hot cup of cocoa! Have a great night, Harvey and Branson—Merry Christmas!!!

Harvey says, "Merry Christmas, and good night to you too, Josh!!! Tell the Mrs. and your uncle Chet hello, and tell him to bring his guitar to the reindeer barn sometime for barnswing night! Nobody plays those Christmas songs like he does!"

Branson the Balladeer also says, "good night Josh— Merry Christmas," and then turns around and says to Harvey, "well Harvey, I think I will get going too, and work on some more of my songs. Got a new Christmas tune goin' round in my head and I want to write it down 'fore I forget it! Merry Christmas, Harvey, and next time I'll stay longer and sing to you some of my originals. My mother thinks they're all great songs."

Harvey says, "Ah…oh…okay, Branson… Sure…Merry Christmas!"

The rest of the elves decide to call it a night, and they all say their good nights to each other and head out to their cottages.

Chapter Nine

Harvey and Santa's trunk of sugar snow.

Harvey giggles to himself about Branson the Balladeer and his songs, but he is thinking more about the Christmas season and starts dancing around singing Christmas songs. All of a sudden, his eyes catch a glimpse of a special trunk that belongs to Santa that is filled with a magical dust called, sugar snow.

Now, sugar snow is special and it only falls at Christmastime, and only at the North Pole's pole. This is what Santa sprinkles on his reindeer every year to cause them to fly. Its magic also makes them to never tire out while they are en route delivering Christmas presents.

Harvey starts to think how wonderful it would be to get into Santa's trunk of sugar snow and put a little bit on his toes to give some spring to his step. *"just enough to make me feel good and tingly but not get caught"* is what he is thinking, but how wrong could one elf be?

He opens Santa's sugar snow trunk and starts putting sugar snow on his toes. He starts to rise, and before he knows it he's 5 feet in the air!

Harvey grabs a post in the stable to pull himself back down, but when he lets go of the post, he immediately rises again and flies even higher!

This happens over and over, and Harvey wishes some of the elves were there to rescue him! He finally decides he can't do anything about it, and starts having fun with the sugar snow. The sugar snowflakes swirl around him, giggling and laughing as they make Harvey ping pong from one end of the stable to the other.

Then Harvey starts singing…

Ha Ha Ha, Ho Ho Ho
I love playing in the sugar snow
just a little bit all sprinkled on my toes
up, up, up and away we go!
Ha Ha Ha, Ho Ho Ho
I love playing in the sugar snow
just a little bit—no one will ever know
that I've been playing in the sugar snow
Ha Ha Ha, Ho Ho Ho
I love playing in the sugar snow
the deer are asleep-and I'm in here all alone
I'm gonna play in the sugar snow

What a sight! Harvey is having the time of his life, but he has forgotten that he left the water hose on at the reindeer water tank. Water is overflowing the tank and runs into each of the reindeer stalls. The deer have gone to sleep and they don't know that they will wake up finding they have slept in a pool of water! And we all know what happens to water at the North Pole— it turns to ice!

After many hours of having fun with the sugar snow, Harvey sees the overflowed water and starts to panic but can't stop himself to turn off the hose!

CHAPTER TEN

Strike the Bell

Now Santa has a friend, who we spoke of earlier whose name is Strike. He is a real Christmas Bell that stands in the middle of Santa's village. His purpose is to alert Santa when a visitor comes to the North Pole, as well as striking when Santa leaves with the reindeer on Christmas eve. Strike also lets Mrs. Santa and all in the village know when Santa and the reindeer return from their Christmas flight.

Strike begins noticing something is wrong over in the reindeer barn. Then he sees it's Harvey flying from one end of it to the other!

During his bouncing, Harvey grabs the front door from the inside. The door opens and all of a sudden, Harvey starts flying outside! He grabs the edge of the front porch and holds on for dear life!

His legs go out and up and all around and he starts hollering for help! Strike immediately starts sounding off to alert Santa that Harvey is in trouble!

Santa, Mrs. Santa, Plum Puddin' and Pinecone hear Strike ringing and rush out of the cottage to see what is the matter. Then they notice Harvey hanging and hollering for help.

They hurry over to Harvey, and Harvey says, "Santa, please forgive me! I got into the sugar snow trunk and I put a bit on my toes to have a little fun, but things got out of control and it wouldn't wear off! I couldn't get to the water hose to turn it off and now the water troughs have all overflowed and the reindeer have been sleeping in water up to their noses! Would you please get me down?"

25

Harvey had forgotten that only Santa can make the sugar snow stops its magic. Otherwise, you have to wait 'till after Christmas for it to wear off.

Then Santa says, "Sugar snow, sugar snow, stop your work, and let him go!"

After Santa says those words, the sugar snow starts swirling around and leaves Harvey. In a big swish, it goes thru the reindeer barn doors and back into Santa's chest with the other sugar snow.

Harvey falls immediately into a big snow pile, but is safe.

Santa, Harvey, and the gang run quickly inside the reindeer barn to turn off the water hose. Then they check each of the reindeer to find them awake but very sick. Laying in their stalls in the water over the hours had given them bad colds, and they are shivering and shaking and sneezing.

Harvey once again panics, realizing they may not be able to pull Santa's sleigh and that it is his fault, and he says, "Santa, whatever shall we do? Can't you fix them? Oh Santa—oh Santa—I am so sorry! Please don't send me away!"

Santa replies, "Harvey, I can do many things but I can't heal humans or animals. Is everything else ready?"

"Yes! Everything is wrapped and the elves have your sleigh loaded. All that is lacking is "only" the sick reindeer! They can hardly move a hoof! I will put blankets on them and give them fresh straw but, Santa, I don't think it will help at all!"

Mrs. Claus tries to comfort Harvey and says, "Harvey, Santa, and I forgive you. We know you didn't mean to do this to the reindeer, and we know you like to have fun. And of course Santa will not send you away for you are the jolliest of the elves and that is one of the things we all love about you. Now stay here in the reindeer barn and keep a watch on the reindeer and keep reporting back to Santa how they are doing so he can figure out what he needs to do in delivering the presents tomorrow night."

"Yes ma'am, Mrs. Claus!" Harvey answers.

Pinecone looks up at Plum Puddin' and barks. Plum Puddin' looks down at Pinecone, knowing what he barked about and then says, "you're right Pinecone, we'll go warm up some plum pudding and bring it back to the sick reindeer."

They all start walking back to Santa's cottage, and Mrs. Claus says, "now, Santa, when we get back to the cottage I'll go make you some hot cocoa and you go relax in your favorite chair and check your list twice and read some of the childrens letters. It always calms you down to read their Christmas wishes."

Santa says, "ok, momma, that and praying that our boys will get well is all I know to do."

When hearing that Santa likes to read children's letters, it makes Plum Puddin' remember that he has Snowdeer's letter he is supposed to give him.

"Santa, I forgot! A special friend of mine, his name is Snowdeer, who is a real solid white young buck who lives with his family in a forest called Doe Run, asked me to deliver this letter to you."

"Why thank you Plum Puddin'. Hum, oh yea I remember Snowdeer and his beautiful white fur! I wonder what our little friend wants for Christmas."

Santa opens Snowdeer's letter, and reads it quietly, and all of a sudden his eyes light up with excitement and he says…

"This is it! Snowdeer will be getting his wish if the reindeer are still sick tomorrow night! Ho Ho Ho!!! Let's go back to the reindeer barn and tell Harvey and the reindeer the great news!"

Santa, Mrs. Santa, Pinecone, and Plum Puddin' go back one more time to the reindeer stalls. They find Harvey sitting with the reindeer— petting and trying to comfort them all. He is still very sad and sorry for what has happened.

Santa goes up to Harvey and says, "Cheer up Harvey! I have great news for you and the reindeer! Listen to this!" Santa tells Harvey and the reindeer about Snowdeer and his special Christmas wish and how he will make Snowdeer's dream come true the next night if they are still sick.

The reindeer, as sick as they are, let Santa know they love his plan. Harvey starts jumping up and down without the help of sugar snow!

Plum Puddin' goes to Santa and Mrs. Santa's cottage to warm up plum pudding, and takes it to the reindeer and then he returns to continue his visit with Santa and Mrs. Santa.

Santa announces, "Well, our new plan will probably go into effect tomorrow night! Santa and Mrs. Santa hug and dance around together when suddenly, Santa stops and says, "Oh no, I just thought of something."

Mrs. Claus asks, "what's that, dear?"

How am I going to get to Snowdeer's home with just the sleigh alone and no reindeer to fly it?"

Pinecone barks and starts scratching on the door. Santa opens the door and Pinecone runs to the front of the sleigh and stands where the reindeer stand when they pull Santa's sleigh. Then Plum Puddin' says, "I guess you got your answer Santa! Pinecone wants to drive your sleigh! Haha"

Santa says, "I do need you to introduce me to Snowdeer and his family so, Plum Puddin', do you mind accompanying me on my sleigh tomorrow night? And Pinecone, will you give me the honor of guiding my sleigh to Doe Run?"

"Yes sir! We would love to ride with you on your sleigh!"

Pinecone barks and jumps with happiness, letting Santa know he would love to pull his sleigh.

"What do you think, Mrs. Claus?"

Mrs. Santa answers, "it is a great idea but you have forgotten something. You need to go to the North Pole marker and gather some "sugar snow" magic dust. New sugar snow is falling and you know how powerful freshly fallen sugar snow can be! Throw some sugar snow on Pinecone and on your sleigh and they will fly you and Plum Puddin' directly to Doe Run, where you can ask Snowdeer if he and the rest of his family would want to pull the sleigh to deliver gifts. Be sure to take your Christmas stocking full of sugar snow along with you-you're going to have a full team pulling your sleigh and you're going to need it. Won't they be surprised Santa!"

A very excited Santa says, "Ho, Ho, Ho... Yes they will! Now, let's go to bed and rest before tomorrow night's takeoff! Plum Puddin', you will stay the night with us and go with us on the flight tomorrow night!"

"Yes sir!"

So they all go to bed...

Chapter Eleven

December 24th

The next day, December 24th, Santa goes to check on the reindeer once again and finds they are still sick. When he returns to his cottage he tells them about his reindeer looking so sad, but then they started grinning when he told them Snowdeer was going to get his Christmas wish and pull his sleigh!

Santa and the gang begin to say yea, and Plum Puddin' says, "this is reason to celebrate! Warm up the Plum Puddin'! Let's eat!! Haha"

Later that evening, when it is close to Santa's time to go deliver gifts, Mrs. Santa, Plum Puddin' and the gang go to the village court yard. They and all the elves gather to watch Santa's takeoff.

Strike the bell, starts ringing his bell using his sound to round up all the elves. They look at each other and whisper amongst themselves, knowing the reindeer are sick. They wonder what Santa will do this year.

Mrs. Claus, Plum Puddin', Pinecone and the others watch Santa as he takes off walking behind their village to the North Pole marker at the top of the world. With his own personal Christmas stocking with a big "SC" on the front, he walks up a hill to the North Pole and looks up to the North Star and begins smiling.

Plum Puddin' rounds up the elf choir and they start singing, *Christmastime/verse of Christmas*. The elves take turns saying, 'C' is for the carols, 'H' is for the holly, 'R' is for the righteous, 'I' is for the incense, and go thru the word Christmas.

Santa kneels down by the North Pole marker, and then looks up at the bright light from the sky that is always shining on the North

Pole. The light beams down even brighter on him and his stocking and the sugar snow magically starts falling faster and faster. Then, all of a sudden, a small blizzard of sugar snow fills his Christmas stocking. Santa gets a big grin and says, "Ho Ho Ho" and Plum Puddin' and the elf choir sing the song, *Christmastime/verse of Christmas* at a higher volume and those watching him from the village start cheering.

Santa gets up and starts walking toward the village. When he comes back he says to Mrs. Santa, Plum Puddin' and all, "I have my stocking full of sugar snow. Now to coat the sleigh and get on our way! Ho Ho Ho!"

The whole North Pole village starts cheering again.

Plum Puddin' says, "Pinecone and I are ready to go, aren't we Pinecone?"

Pinecone barks and takes his spot at the front of the sleigh, wearing a special harness that Harvey just made.

Harvey goes up to Santa and whispers in his ear that the reindeer are still sick. Plum Puddin' gets in Santa's sleigh and then Santa steps in his sleigh. Before sitting down he announces, "The reindeer are still sick and Plum Puddin' is going to guide me and Pinecone is going to fly me to a special friend by the name of Snowdeer who lives in Doe Run. He and his family are going to guide my sleigh to deliver the gifts tonight to all the children and animals in the world!"

The elves all cheer and throw their hats in the air! Santa gives Mrs. Claus a kiss on the cheek then he takes his stocking full of sugar snow and starts putting some of its magic dust on Pinecone and his sleigh. They immediately start to rise off the ground and Santa has to hurry and sit down so he doesn't fall out of his sleigh!

Santa gives the command, "Ho-Ho-Ho! Take me to Doe Run," and the sleigh takes off in a rush.

Everyone cheers again and in only a matter of minutes Santa arrives at Doe Run at the Jim-Buck family cottage in the woods.

Chapter Twelve

Santa meets the Jim-Buck family

Santa goes up to the front door and knocks and says, "Ho Ho Ho! Is anybody home?"

Jim-Buck peeks out the front door. When he realizes it is Santa along with Plum Puddin' and Pinecone, he can't believe his eyes. Then he says, "Oh!!! Is it really you, Santa?"

Santa replies, "yes it is me, Jim-Buck! All my reindeer have taken sick and we need you to join our team to pull the sleigh to deliver gifts. You see I got a letter from a certain member of your family who wishes to help me tonight! Ho Ho Ho"

Jim-buck says, "wow! Is Snowdeer going to be happy! He went to bed real early tonight. I bet he is dreaming that he is pulling your sleigh. I'll go wake him, Santa. I can't wait for him to see you."

Jim-buck goes to Snowdeer's bedroom, where Snowdeer is fast asleep and says, "wake up Snowdeer! There is a very special guest here to see you."

Snowdeer says, "who is it, daddy?"

"Well, come and see- it's a surprise."

Snowdeer, being half-awake, comes to the front door and sees Santa, Plum Puddin', Pinecone and the sleigh. He stands, staring at them, thinking he is still dreaming, when all of a sudden Santa says, "Snowdeer, all my reindeer have taken ill, and I need you to pull my sleigh. Can you help us?"

Snowdeer, realizing he is not dreaming says, "can I help you? Santa, that was my Christmas wish I sent you and you got it! Santa, I would be honored to help pull your sleigh! Can my family go too?"

Snowdeer sees Pinecone still rising up off the ground in front of the sleigh and he says, "Santa, I didn't know Pinecone could fly!"

Santa looks over at Pinecone and realizes the sugar snow still has a hold of him. Then Santa laughs and says, "Ho Ho Ho! I forgot! Sugar snow! Sugar snow! Stop your work and let him go!"

Pinecone immediately drops safely into the snow as the sugar snow swirls around and goes back into Santa's stocking with the 'SC' on it.

Santa says, "now, back to your question Snowdeer, why sure your family can go! You asked for that in your letter, and Santa is going to make your Christmas wish come true! Now get harnessed up and let's take off! We have a busy night ahead of us my little deer! Ho Ho Ho!"

Snowdeer can't believe his ears and says, "wow, even Santa said *my little deer* to me! Oh well, let's get ready for take off! There are a lot of boys and girls and animals to deliver presents to."

Santa harnesses Snowdeer's family to his sleigh. They all stand so proud and tall in their flight gear ready for takeoff. But, Santa has one more thing to do before he starts their flight, and he says to them, "I need to cover you all with magical snow dust from the North Pole that we call sugar snow. It will keep you flying and you will never get tired and we will get all of the Christmas gifts delivered in time!"

"Isn't this cool," said Snowdeer. "See, any Christmas wish can come true! It's "happy hoof dance" time! Hahaha"

Snowdeer and his family all shout with joy and go into the happy hoof dance. Then Santa goes to each deer and begins to throw magical sugar snow dust over them. Suddenly, they start to rise straight up in the air! Santa hops into his sleigh but right before he calls them to take off, Snowdeer looks at his family and then at Santa and says, "Merry Christmas everybody! I love that wonderful Christmas time of year!" Santa couldn't agree more and says, "me too Snowdeer, me too! So, Ho Ho Ho, let's go!"

CHAPTER THIRTEEN

Santa makes Snowdeer's dream come true

Santa, Snowdeer, Plum Puddin' and all take off in Santa's sleigh and fly away. Only this time Pinecone sits with Santa and Plum Puddin' in the sleigh. They are all flying and laughing delivering gifts all night long.

They are amazed at the view they have from the air and how they didn't get tired! When they got the last gift delivered, Santa tells them to start flying north to the North Pole.

They are thrilled to get to go where Santa lives! As they arrive at the North Pole they hear Strike the bell and thousands of elves welcoming them.

Mrs. Santa has arranged for the greatest Christmas celebration ever at the North Pole. She has gifts for all of them and a lot of plum pudding for Plum Puddin'. They have hundreds of trees decorated in beautiful Christmas lights. The trees are decorated with fruit, berries, nuts and whatever else the deer can feast on. They sing Christmas carols around the trees like Deerlores did when she was a little doe, and they even danced the happy hoof dance!

When they started that, Harvey grabbed some sugar snow from Santa's sock and threw it on himself and started ping ponging again. But this time he knew Santa wouldn't care because it was Christmas!

The reindeer were over their colds, and joined the Jim-Buck family in the happy hoof dance and eating the goodies from the trees.

Plum Puddin' goes up to Santa and says, "Santa, thank you so very much for everything. This is my best Christmas ever. If you wouldn't mind, could I ask for two more things please?"

"What is that, Plum Puddin'?"

"Would you magically bring my mom, Rose Marie and daddy Darrell here? Also, I told Snowdeer I would ask you if every year when I come here with my special magical jar of plum pudding, could I bring Snowdeer too?"

Santa happily says, "Ho Ho Ho, your wishes are granted! Bringing everyone together into the family is what Christmas is all about!"

A very grateful Snowdeer says, "oh, thank you Santa! Thank you! If you give me a magical jar like you gave Plum Puddin', I promise to bring it full of mixed nuts and berries for you every year!"

Santa gives a big Ho Ho Ho and they all laugh at what Snowdeer said.

While Plum Puddin' is laughing, he happens to look over at the North Pole's pole and sees his mama Rose Marie and daddy Darrell appearing. They look around in wonder at Santa's village.

When they see Plum Puddin' they all run toward each other and hug and laugh in delight. While Snowdeer is watching this take place, he all of a sudden sees a magical jar at his hoofs with the same brightness of Plum Puddins' jar. But this jar has a golden lid with a green 'S' for Santa on it. Then Snowdeer says, "Oh, wow Santa, you did it! Thank you, thank you very much! Me and this jar will be seeing you every Christmas from now on!"

Santa, not passing up an opportunity to pick at Snowdeer says, "I'll be watching for you-my little deer! Ho Ho Ho!"

Snowdeer gets that *"oh no, not again, he called me little deer"* look, but then quickly starts laughing and goes into the happy hoof dance.

CHAPTER FOURTEEN

Grandpa Deer's special secret

Grandpa Deer closes the book and says, "well, there's a deer Christmas story if I ever heard one! Hahaha. It was one happy Christmas eve night for Snowdeer and the Jim-Buck family, and their best Christmas day ever! Snowdeer got his wish, the reindeer got well, and Snowdeer's family and Plum Puddin's family had finally got together again. And they continue that tradition to this day! Never was there two happier families than these. But, there is still one more secret left to this deer Christmas story."

Young deer, one of Grandpa Deer's granddoe's says, "what is this secret, Grandpa Deer?"

Grandpa deer replies, "all you young bucks and does know me as grandpa—your mother's and father's all know me as Snowdeer!"

On that very special night, reindeer couldn't make their flight—but my wish Santa did hear, and he chose me—for I'm Snowdeer!

The End

ABOUT THE AUTHOR

Randy Plummer is a singer, songwriter and bass player in Branson, Missouri. He, along with his parents, Darrell & Rosie Plummer and sister Melody started the 3rd family theatre in Branson in 1973 until 1990, called, *The Plummer Family Country Music Show*. SNOWDEER is his first book and is also being performed as a Production in Branson.

Randy Plummer has SNOWDEER as a 2 Disc Set for sale. One Disc is the SNOWDEER Story and the 2nd Disc is 10 tracks featuring songs from the SNOWDEER Story. Please write Randy at Box 1144, Branson, MO 65615 or e-mail Randy at:

plumpuddin@tri-lakes.net

www.randyplummer.com

Continue reading for poems and lyrics featured on the Snowdeer Two-Disk set

SNOWDEER'S POEM

This story's about Snowdeer

Only 7 years old

Who has a great big story to tell

That never has been told

His daddy Jim-Buck

And mother Deerlores

With all the family

Live in a place called Doe Run

In a cabin in the woods by the creek

Snowdeer has a Christmas wish

That he has wished all year

And that's to pull ole Santa's sleigh

With all the family deer

He wrote a letter to Santa

Sent it to the North Pole

With dreams that Santa reads it

And grants all that it holds

Santa finally sees it

Tho' there'd been a delay

For when his reindeer all took sick

Ole Snowdeer got his way

Then Santa flew to Doe Run

With help of sugar snow

To meet the Jim-Buck family

And deliver his load

The thrill that Snowdeer felt

When Santa Claus had come

Was one that he'd never forget

It was second to none

This was Snowdeer's best Christmas

Both Christmas Eve and Day

To celebrate the greatest season

That could ever come his way

This story's happy ending

Gives hope to all who read

For Santa grants the wishes

To all who do believe

I'M HAVING CHRISTMAS ON THE INSIDE

1

I know it's not quite Christmas yet
But inside me I dream
Of gathering with friends and family
—all that's dear to me
I just can't wait to hear those carols
From the hearts of those who sing
I'm getting ready for it to come
And everything it brings

Chorus

I'm having Christmas on the inside
I don't need a candles glow
Or a stoney fireplace brimmed with firewood
Or the sight of fallen snow
I'm having Christmas on the inside
That's God's special gift to me
And sharing faith and hope and love
With my family

2

It's not December 25th
But that's alright with me
For I don't need a calendar
To know what Christmas means
That warm exciting feeling in me
I carry all year long
I'm getting ready for it to come
Sing with me on this song

Chorus

Bridge

For Christmas day will not be long
And the best is yet to come
When I feel the hope and cheer
That Christmas brings and gives me here

Chorus

MERRY, MERRY, MERRY, MERRY CHRISTMAS TO YOU

D.O.C. SEPT. 7, 2003

Chorus

Merry, merry, merry, merry Christmas to you
Hope all your seasons dreams come true
May your Christmas be white not blue
Merry, merry, merry, merry Christmas to you
I know this saying is not new
Merry, merry, merry, merry Christmas to you

1

You told me last year you were pretty bad
And you done some things that were pretty sad
But I can't see that comin' from you
So, wipe that slate and make it clean as new
Ole Santa won't leave a lump of coal-no do
So, merry, merry, merry, merry Christmas to you

Chorus

2

Santa won't take you off his list
So, come here baby and give me a kiss
You're near 'bout perfect as I've ever seen
And you'll always be the one of my dreams
Me and ole Santa like the things you do
So, merry, merry, merry, merry Christmas to you

42

Chorus

3

Tonight let's go out and have some fun
And deck the halls 'till 12 or 1
Build a snowman in the yard
And make snow angels till we're good and tired
Christmas Cheer's addicting it's true
So, merry, merry, merry, merry Christmas to you

Chorus

HA-HA-HA-HO-HO-HO

(Harvey The Elf's Song)

D.O.C. June 2011

Ha Ha Ha-Ho Ho Ho

I love playing in the sugar snow

Just a little bit all sprinkled on my toes

Up up up and away we go!

Ha Ha Ha-Ho Ho Ho

I love playing in the sugar snow

Just a little bit-no one will ever know

That I've been playing in the sugar snow

Ha Ha Ha-Ho Ho Ho

I love playing in the sugar snow

The deer are asleep and I'm in here all alone

I'm gonna play in the sugar snow

THAT WONDERFUL CHRISTMAS TIME OF YEAR

1

It's a time of laughter, it's a time of singing
It's that wonderful Christmas time of year
It's the time when we all get with our families
and have fellowship with ones that we hold dear
It's a great time-and the Season
to make memories that will last for years and years
So, let's all sing and make memories now
Makin' memories in that wonderful Christmas time of year

2

It's a time of giving, not just receiving
It's a time to show great love to everyman
So, let's all pitch in and do our part now
trying to do as much as we possibly can
All the presents, the cards and greetings
gives us things we can think about throughout the year
So, let's all give and make memories now
Makin' memories in that wonderful Christmas time of year

Chorus
It's the time to remember the Christ Child
born of Mary with Joseph from Galilee
It's the time of year we all should thank God for sending Jesus
and for the blessings that we all receive
For without Him, there's be no reason
to celebrate this great Holiday
So, lift up your voices—sing loud for all to hear
As we celebrate that wonderful Christmas time of year

STRIKE THE BELL

D.O.C. June 20, 2011

1

Harvey has a problem

He must let Santa know

He disobeyed and got in Santa's trunk of sugar snow

He put a little bit upon the tops of all his toes

And now he ping-pongs at the reindeer barn out of control

Chorus

Strike the bell! Strike the bell!

Let Santa know things are not well

Strike the bell! Strike the bell!

Ring loud and clear about Harvey Elf

2

Harvey's hangin' on the roof

He can't come down you see

And only Santa can make it stop

With magic words he speaks

For anyone who plays in sugar snow

'Fore Christmas eve

Will be under it's magic

Until after Christmas leaves

46

Chorus

3

Strike is Santa's buddy

He hangs there all year long

And if he sees a problem

You'll hear him ding and dong

But mostly he rings loudly

When it is Christmas eve

When Santa takes off with his reindeer

You can hear him leave

Chorus

CHRISTMAS TIME/VERSE OF CHRISTMAS

D.O.C 8/8/11

Chorus

Christmas time, Christmas time

I love the Christmas time

Christmas time, Christmas time

I wait all year for

Christmas time, Christmas time

Love when it's Christmas time

Love all the things

This season holds dear

1st verse of Christmas

C is for the carols we sing at Christmas time

H is for the holly leaves and berries all entwined

R is for the reindeer that pull ole Santa's sleigh

I is for the incense that burns so sweet of sage

S is for the shopping for presents we will give

T is for the time we spend giving of these gifts

M is for the mothers and fathers whom we love

For they're the ones who taught us all about God's love

A is for the apple -the apple of God's eye and He is...

S the Savior-born that Christmas night

48

2nd verse of Christmas

C is for Jesus' crib where the star shown down so bright

H is for the hay Jesus lay upon that night

R is for the route the wise men took to find the King

I is for the importance that knowing Jesus brings

S is for the stable-the lowly place he stayed

T is for the travels to Bethlehem they made

M is for the magi who came with gifts to bring-

Gold, frankincense and myrrh to lay at Jesus' feet

A is for the anthem to Jesus we will sing

S is for the Son of God who gives life true meaning

3rd verse of Christmas

C is for the Christ, born of Mary, Son of Man

H is for the humble beginnings Jesus had

R is for the righteous who place their faith in him

I is for Israel-the place it all began

S is for shalom-a greeting known to Israel

T is for glad tidings Jesus brought to all the world

M is for the manger-the place he laid his head

For there was no room in the inn, no vacancy, no bed

A is for the angels who appeared in Bethlehem to…

S for shepherds saying, "Peace on Earth good will toward men"

RANDY PLUMMER

P.O. BOX 1144

BRANSON, MO 65615

plumpuddin@tri-lakes.net

www.randyplummer.com